S0-AEB-318

Tenni

• An Introduction to Being a Good Sport •

by Aaron Derr
illustrations by Scott Angle

Start Smart books are published by Red Chair Press
Red Chair Press LLC PO Box 333 South Egremont, MA 01258-0333
www.redchairpress.com

Publisher's Cataloging-In-Publication Data

Names: Derr, Aaron. | Angle, Scott, illustrator.

Title: Tennis : an introduction to being a good sport / by Aaron Derr ; illustrations by Scott Angle.

Description: South Egremont, MA : Red Chair Press, [2017] | Start smart: sports | Interest age level: 005-009. | Includes Fast Fact sidebars, a glossary and references for additional reading. | Includes bibliographical references and index. | Summary: "Playing a sport is good exercise and fun, but playing the game is more fun for everyone when you know the rules of the game and how to be a good sport. Tennis is one of the most popular sports for both young and old alike. In this book, readers learn the history of the game, the rules of play and how to score in this fun and wacky racquet sport."-- Provided by publisher.

Identifiers: LCCN 2016934117 | ISBN 978-1-63440-133-3 (library hardcover) | ISBN 978-1-63440-139-5 (paperback) | ISBN 978-1-63440-145-6 (ebook)

Subjects: LCSH: Tennis--Juvenile literature. | Sportsmanship--Juvenile literature. CYAC: Tennis. | Sportsmanship.

Classification: LCC GV996.5 .D47 2017 (print) | LCC GV996.5 (ebook) | DDC 796.342--dc23

Illustration credits: Scott Angle; technical charts by Joe LeMonnier

Photo credits: Cover p. 8, 13, 14, 20, 22, 27, 28, 30, 31: Dreamstime; p. 32: Courtesy of the author, Aaron Derr

This series first published by:
Red Chair Press LLC PO Box 333 South Egremont, MA 01258-0333

Printed in the United States of America

Distributed in the U.S. by Lerner Publisher Services. www.lernerbooks.com

1116 1P CGBS17

Table of Contents

Words in **bold type** are defined in the glossary.

First Lesson

Ella and Evan are at their first tennis lesson. Their coach spent the first part of the class teaching them about the rules. Then they learned how to hit the ball.

Now, they're finally ready to play a real game. Ella smacks the ball over the net. It bounces on Evan's side, but when he tries to hit it back, it goes **out of bounds**.

Ella gets a point!

“15-**love**,” says the coach.

“Whaaaaat?!?” Ella and Evan say at the same time.

“That’s how you keep score in tennis,” their coach says. “It’s a little bit different than other sports.”

“Okaaaaay,” Ella and Evan say at the same time.

When the game starts again, Ella gets another point.

“30-love,” says the coach.

Ella and Evan look at each other. Looks like they have a lot to learn!

FUN FACT

The earliest version of tennis was played 900 years ago. Back then, players didn’t use **rackets***. They used their hands!

*often spelled racquet

CHAPTER 2 Serve it Up

Before their first lesson, Ella and Evan didn't know much about tennis.

"I bet I know more than you!" said Ella. "I'm pretty sure I know more than you!" said Evan.

They knew that one player tried to hit the ball over the net, and the other player tried to hit it back. And they knew the ball couldn't bounce twice on the same side or go out of bounds. But that's about all they knew!

Their coach taught them that every tennis game begins with a **serve**. The serving player has to stand at the very back of the court. Then he has to hit the ball diagonally over the net onto the other side of the court. (See page 11)

JUST JOKING!

Q: What number comes before tennis?

A: Nine-is!

If the server is standing on the right side of the court, the serve has to cross over the net and land on the left side of the court. If the server is standing on the left, the ball has to land on the right side of the court.

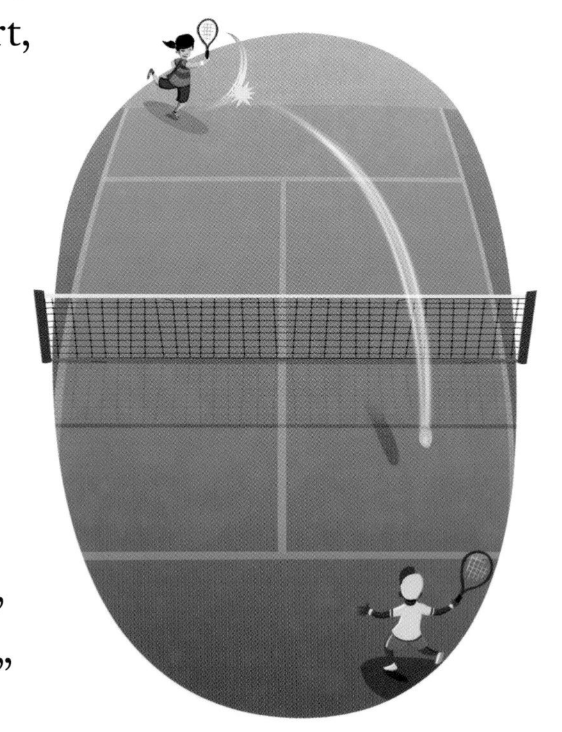

"I already knew that!" Evan said. "You did not!" Ella said.

FUN FACT

Tennis players serve **overhand.** After that, most shots are either **forehand** or **backhand.** A forehand shot begins on the same side of your body as the hand you use naturally. For example, if you're right-handed, a forehand shot begins on your right. A backhand shot begins on the opposite side across your body. Both are important skills!

It was Ella's turn to try first. Since she's right-handed, she tossed the ball up in the air with her left hand. When the ball was high enough in the air, she swung the racket with her right hand.

Boom! The ball soared over the net and landed right where she wanted it to bounce.

"Great serve, Ella!" Evan said.

JUST JOKING!

Q: Why do tennis players make good waiters?

A: They're always serving!

After the serve, tennis players can hit the ball wherever they want to, as long as it goes over the net, and as long as it lands inside the lines.

The goal is to hit the ball far enough away from the other player so she can't hit it back. But you also can't hit it too far or it will go out of bounds. If the ball bounces twice on your side, the other player gets the point!

DID YOU KNOW?

Tennis can be played indoors or outdoors. It can be played on natural grass or on an **artificial surface**. The size of the court is the same no matter what. So what's with all the different lines? The boundaries—what's "in bounds" and what's "out of bounds"—are different depending on how many people are playing. When two people are playing against each other it's called singles, and the playing area is smaller. When four people are playing—two against two—it's called doubles, and the playing area is bigger. That's why there are so many confusing lines on a tennis court!

ON THE COURT!

To begin, the server stands behind the baseline and serves the ball to the service box diagonally across the court. The server has two attempts to put the ball in play. If on the first serve, the ball tips the net but falls on the other side, this is a "let" and the server gets another chance at the first serve. During Play: If the ball lands on the inside edge of the white line is it in bounds or out of bounds? If the ball touches any part of the white sideline, the ball is out-of-bounds.

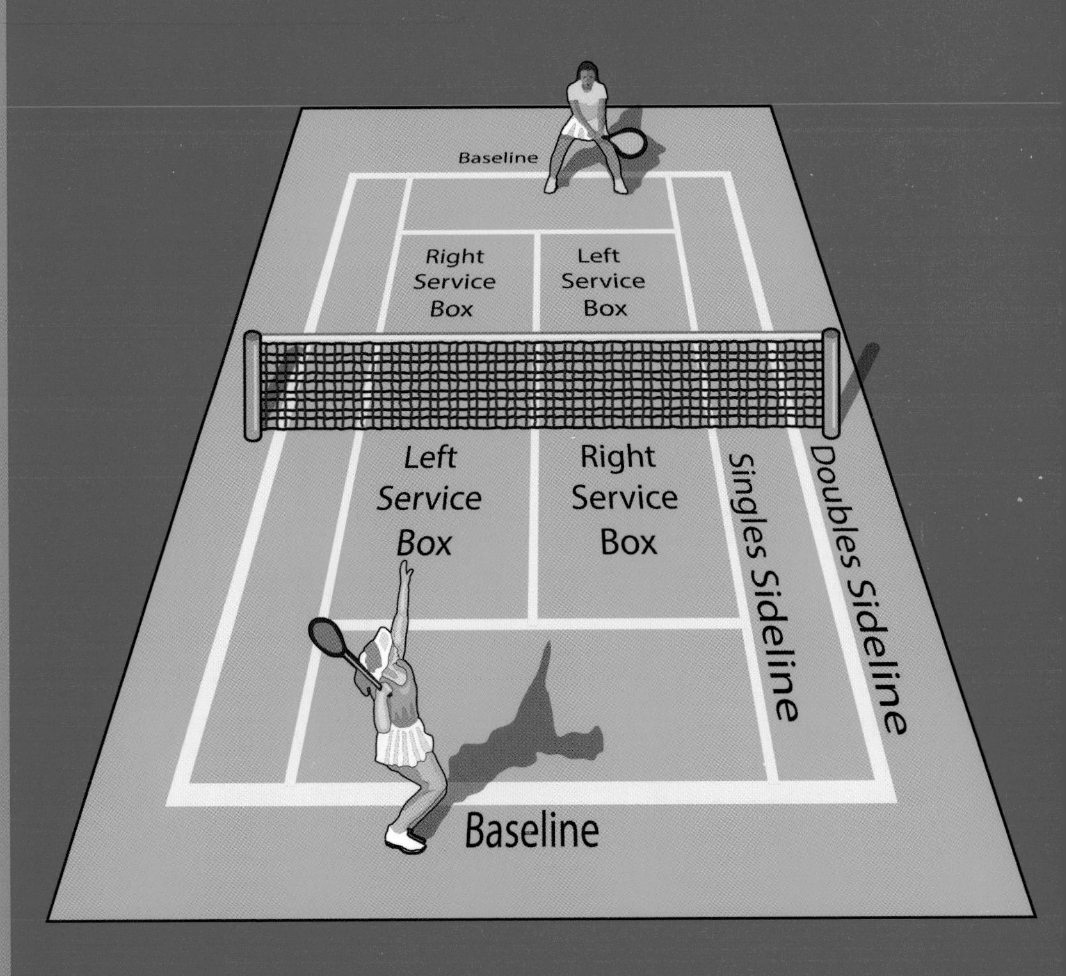

CHAPTER 3

Game, Set, Match

Now that they know the basics, Evan and Ella are playing their first game. This is when tennis gets *really* interesting.

When you have zero points in a tennis game, your score is called “love.” When you win your first point, you have “15.” So when Ella wins the first point against Evan, the score is 15-love.

When you win a second point, your score is “30.”

"I already know what comes next," says Evan. "When you win your third point, it's called '45,' right?"

"Not exactly," their coach says. "When you score the third point, it's called '40.' "

"I already knew that!" Ella says.

"You did not!" Evan says.

FUN FACT

The four Grand Slam **tournaments** are the most important tennis events in the world. They are the Australian Open, the French Open, Wimbledon and the U.S. Open.

"The first player to win four points wins the game," their coach says. "Unless both players have won three points. That's called '**deuce**.' Then you have to win by two points in order to win the game."

"Oh brother!" Evan says.

The score is 40-30, and Ella is winning. She needs to win just one more point to win the game. Ella hits the best serve of her life, and Evan can't get to it in time. This is called an **ace**. Ella wins the game!

DID YOU KNOW?

The part of the tennis racket that hits the ball is called the strings. Its works a lot like a trampoline, only it's much, much smaller! When the ball hits the strings, it bounces off, much like your body bounces on a trampoline. But a tennis ball moves way faster. Many professional players can make the ball go faster than 100 miles per hour! Now that's fast!

“Great game, Evan,” she says. “Good game, Ella,” says Evan.

“Hey guys, you aren’t done yet,” their coach says. “You finished the game, but you haven’t finished the **set**.”

“I already knew that!” Evan says. “You did not!” Ella says.

Most tennis events have more than one game. A set is a group of games played one after the other between the same two players. The players take turns serving for each game.

Since Ella served the first game, Evan gets to serve the second. Today, whoever wins two out of three games wins the set.

In most adult professional tournaments, the first player to win six games wins the set.

"Unless *both players* have won five games," their coach says. "Then a player has to win by two games in order to win the set."

"Gee, I didn't know that!" Ella says.

JUST JOKING!

Q: Why don't tennis players like Valentine's Day?

A: Because 'love' stinks!

Game After Game

Evan has worked hard on his serves. He hits the ball hard and it almost always lands in just the right spot.

But Ella has been working hard, too. She races back and forth across the court to hit the ball back to Evan.

Evan hits the ball back to Ella, and it lands right on the white line before bouncing past Ella.

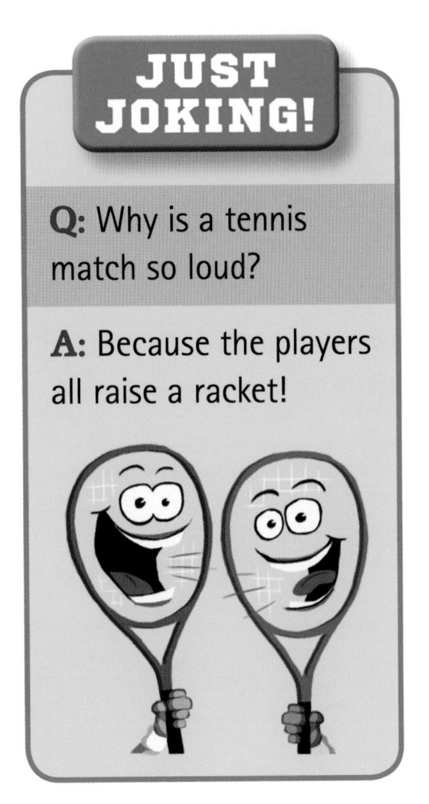

"Out!" says Ella. "In!" says Evan.

"Actually," their coach says, "Evan is right. When the ball hits the line, it counts as in."

"I knew that!" says Evan.

"Good shot, Evan," Ella says.

Evan eventually wins the second game, and that means he wins the first set.

DID YOU KNOW?

You don't have to let the ball bounce before you return it to your opponent. A volley is a shot made before the ball hits the ground. Sometimes, really good tennis players will run up to the net and hit a volley when the other player is still expecting the ball to bounce on the court.

"Yes!" he says. "It's over! I win!"

"Not quite," says their coach. "You finished the set, but you haven't finished the **match**."

"Bet you didn't know that," Ella says.

"Whoever wins the most sets wins the match," says their coach. "The first player to win 3 sets wins today's match."

Evan and Ella go back and forth. Sometimes he wins, and sometimes she wins.

By the time the match is done, they're super tired.

"Great match, Ella," he says.

"Good match, Evan," she says.

RULES OF THE GAME

When adults and older kids play, the winner must win 5 out of 7 games to win a set. The match is won by the first player to win 3 or 5 sets.

"Good job, guys," their coach says. "You both did great today."

Their coach tells them that it's good to not try to hit the ball too hard when you're first learning how to play tennis. It's more important to be able to control where it goes.

The more and more you practice, the harder you'll be able to hit it. And eventually you'll be able to aim it just right and hit it hard!

DID YOU KNOW?

Most tennis shots are fast and low, except for the lob. The lob is when you hit the ball high on purpose. For example, if the other player has charged the net to hit a volley, you might try to lob it over the player's head to get a point!

"Tomorrow, we'll play doubles," their coach says.

"Whaaaat?!?" Evan and Ella say.

"Does that mean we have to play twice as much?" Evan asks.

"No," their coach says. "It means you play with two people on a team against two other players."

The same basic rules apply when you play doubles instead of singles. Only this time, there's double the amount of players!

"That should be fun!" says Ella.

Doubled Up

The next day, Ella and Evan play a doubles match against two other kids.

Ella serves first, but the player on the other team hits it right back. Ella and Evan both race over to the same spot to hit the ball back.

Evan gets there first and hits the ball over the net, but the other team hits it back again. Only this time, neither Ella nor Evan can get to it in time.

When you're playing with a teammate, you have to work together, even talk to each other on the court. If one player runs over to hit the ball, the other player has to stay in his area in case the ball comes to him next.

"OK, Evan," Ella says. "I'll cover this side, and you cover that side."

"Got it!" Evan says.

The more Evan and Ella play together, the better they get. When one of them hits the ball, the other one gets ready in case the other team hits it right back.

In the final point of the match, Ella smashes the ball over the net, and the other team can't reach it. Ella and Evan win!

"Great job working together, guys," their coach says. "That's what it takes to win at tennis."

"We already knew that!" Evan and Ella say together.

JUST JOKING!

Q: What did one tennis ball say to the other?

A: See you 'round!

What Did You Learn?

See how much you learned about tennis. Answer *true* or *false* for each statement below. Write your answers on a separate piece of paper.

1. A score of zero is called "deuce."
   True or false?

2. The boundaries on a tennis court are different for singles and doubles.
   True or false?

3. The competition is over when a player wins a set.
   True or false?

4. When the ball hits the line, it is considered "in."
   True or false?

5. A lob shot goes high in the air.
   True or false?

Answers: 1. False. (A score of zero is called "love."), 2. True, 3. False. (The competition is over when a player wins the match.), 4. True, 5. True.

For More Information

Books

Egart, Patricia. *Let's Play Tennis! A Guide for Parents and Kids by Andy Ace, 2nd Edition.* Amber Skye Publishing, 2013.

Mantell, Paul. *Arthur Ashe: Young Tennis Champion.* Aladdin Paperbacks, 2006.

Peters, Gregory N. *Serena & Venus Williams Tennis Stars (Trailblazers).* Capstone Press, 2013.

White, Stephen. *Bring Your Racquet: Tennis Basics for Kids.* Kirk House Publishers, 2010.

Places

International Tennis Hall of Fame, Newport, Rhode Island.

Aviva Centre, Toronto, ON, Canada
Stade Uniprix, Montreal, QC, Canada,
Sites of the Rogers Cup Canadian Open Tournament.

Billy Jean King National Tennis Center, New York, New York.
Site of the U.S. Open Tournament.

Web Sites

Rules and information on young peoples' tennis from the US governing body of Tennis
https://www.usta.com/Youth-Tennis

Tennis drills for kids
http://www.tenniscompanion.org/12-essential-tennis-drills-for-beginners-and-kids

New to Kids Tennis? Comprehensive information for kids everywhere
http://www.tenniscanada.com/kids/what-is-kids-tennis

Note to educators and parents: Our editors have carefully reviewed these web sites to ensure they are suitable for children. Web sites change frequently, however, and we cannot guarantee that a site's future contents will continue to meet our high standards of quality and educational value. You may wish to preview these sites and closely supervise children whenever they access the Internet.

Index

About the Author

Aaron Derr Aaron Derr is a writer based just outside of Dallas, Texas. He has more than 15 years of experience writing and editing magazines and books for kids of all ages. When he's not reading or writing, Aaron enjoys watching and playing sports, and being a good sport with his wife and two kids.